This Book Belongs To:

The Little Red Wagon

Billy Jo pulled a small carrot out of the ground. "When are they going to get big?" she asked Benson. It was the bunny's first year growing her own carrots.

"Looks like your carrots just need a little more time," the little bear said.

"Who has time? I'm hungry now. But I suppose you're right," she unhappily admitted.

"How about a lemonade break?" Benson suggested. Then, he saw something red under a pile of twigs and leaves. "What's this?" he asked, going over to pull it out from the rubbish.

"That old thing?" Billy Jo replied. "Just an old wagon. Not good for much of anything."

"Looks like it just needs a little fixing," Benson replied.

"Who has time to fix that?" Billy Jo said.

"I do," Benson replied. "I've always wanted a wagon."

"It's yours," Billy Jo offered, glad to be rid of it.

The next day, Benson went to Randall Raccoon's. Randall collected all kinds of things and searched through his piles of junk until he found the right part for Benson's wagon.

Benson spent all week cleaning, sanding, and painting the little red wagon until it looked almost brand new.

"That's a beautiful wagon, Benson," said Sherry Squirrel. "I bet it could carry a lot of nuts. I found a tree with the most delicious nuts."

"How about we go over and collect them now?" Benson suggested and the two headed off toward the tree.

On the way home, Sherry rode on top of the nuts in the wagon. "Many thanks to you and your wagon, Benson," she said. "It would have taken me a long time to carry all these nuts by myself."

The next day, Bobby Beaver came by. He wanted to use Benson's wagon to help carry his wood. Benson was happy to help.

Bobby and Benson were piling wood onto the wagon when Billy Jo spotted them. "Where'd you get a good wagon like that?" she asked them.

"It's the same one you gave me," Benson answered.

"It looks brand new!" Billy Jo said, surprised. "Look at all the wood it holds. I have plenty of carrots to move. Your wagon would sure help."

"With three of us working, we'll be done with this wood in no time," said Benson.

Once the red wagon was empty, Billy Jo hurried home with it. She carried as many of her now fat carrots as she could at one time and then loaded them onto the wagon. The pile grew and grew until it was quite high.

From a distance, Benson saw the little red wagon straining with the weight of its load. "Stop!" he called. "That's too heavy."

"It's fine," Billy Jo scoffed. So up on top of the pile, she tossed the last of her carrots.

Snap! Off broke one of the tires. *Crash!* The huge pile of carrots came crashing to the ground.

"Oh no!" Benson cried.

"Sorry Benson. I guess you were right about it being too heavy," Billy Jo said.

It took them many trips to pick up all of the carrots and carry them to Billy Jo's burrow.

Benson tried his best to reattach the wheel, but athough it stayed on, it wobbled horribly. He went back to see Randall, and luckily he had a good wheel.

Benson fixed the red wagon and took the Mouse Family Morganson for a ride the next day. It was the children's very first trip to town and they waved at everyone from the wagon.

Benson lent out his wagon to whomever asked, even Billy Jo. To Benson, helping his friends was the best part of having the little red wagon.